The Lost D
MONTEZU
SOOTHSAYER

Also by Clive Dickinson
The Lost Diary of Tutankhamun's Mummy

Other Lost Diaries recently discovered:
The Lost Diary of Henry VIII's Executioner
The Lost Diary of Erik Bloodaxe, Viking Warrior
The Lost Diary of Julius Caesar's Slave
The Lost Diary of Queen Victoria's Undermaid
The Lost Diary of Hercules' Personal Trainer

The Lost Diary of
MONTEZUMA'S
SOOTHSAYER

Found by Clive Dickinson
Illustrated by George Hollingworth

Collins
An imprint of HarperCollins*Publishers*

First published in Great Britain by Collins in 1999

Collins is an imprint of HarperCollins*Publishers* Ltd,
77-85 Fulham Palace Road, Hammersmith, London W6 8JB

1 3 5 7 9 8 6 4 2

Text copyright © Clive Dickinson 1999
Illustrations copyright © George Hollingworth 1999

ISBN 0 00 694587 2

The author asserts the moral right to be
identified as the author of this work

Printed and bound in Great Britain by
Caledonian International Book Manufacturing Ltd, Glasgow, G64

MESSAGE TO READERS

During a recent holiday in Spain, Clive Dickinson and his family visited a local market. Among the stalls selling fruit and vegetables, clothes, shoes, sunglasses and beachwear, his two children found a stall selling postcards and old books. One particular book was made up of pages stitched together so that it opened up like a concertina. There were no written words. Instead the pages were covered in brightly coloured pictures. It looked like a battered old comic book and so ancient that Mr Dickinson thought it might be a rare treasure – a priceless document. Could it have been something brought back to Spain by the early Spanish adventurers in Central America? Further investigation proved that it was.

Leading experts in the history of America before the Spanish conquest carefully examined the book, or codex, as they called it. Dr Shady Practice and Professor Pulltheotherone confirmed that it dated from the early sixteenth century; the time when Spanish soldiers, traders and missionaries had begun to explore and conquer the New World.

The two historians revealed an even more amazing secret. It appeared that the book was a diary, covering the last years of the Aztec empire during the reign of Montezuma II (or Moctezuma, as his name is sometimes spelt) who was the Aztec king, or Great Speaker. When the diary was translated it told of the arrival of Hernán Cortés and the first Spaniards to the Aztec world.

The diarist seems to have been one of the advisers to Montezuma, who had the job of looking into the future to foretell what might happen.

Extracts from the diary appear here for the first time. They give a remarkable picture of the Aztec world and the coming of the Spanish invaders who would soon conquer it.

Note: The diarist, Guessalotl, used the system of dates in the Aztec farming calendar. This had eighteen months. Each month was twenty days long and there were five days left over at the end of the year. However, to make it easier to follow, the translation printed here uses dates in the Christian calendar.

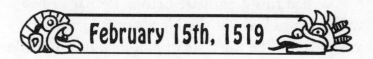

February 15th, 1519

The second day of the first month of the Aztec year

I had a nightmare last night. As I lay on my reed sleeping mat wrapped in my cloak, I dreamt I heard a voice saying: 'Fasten your seat-belt, please, Señor Guessalotl. We'll be landing in Mexico City soon.'

I've had this nightmare before. Perhaps I had too much *pulque** at the New Year's Day party yesterday. I like the taste of *pulque* but it must do strange things to my head. I'd better watch out. The law is very strict about drinking too much. Only old people are allowed to get drunk. The law says that younger people who get drunk will be sentenced to death. There's enough sentencing to death as it is and I don't want to end up as another human sacrifice to the gods – even for the sake of an extra cup of *pulque*.

That was another thing about my nightmare. There wasn't any *pulque*. In fact there wasn't much that I could recognize at all. I seemed to be sitting in a huge round pipe – like a giant reed, only it was made of a shiny metal, a bit like silver. There were other people sitting around me in rows. We were all facing the same way and the person in front was sitting so close my knees were touching the back of his seat.

*alcoholic drink made from cactus juice

But the worst part of the nightmare was when I turned to one side. There was a hole in the side of the pipe. Looking through this I could see the mountains around the city. There was no mistaking them; I'd know them anywhere. The frightening part was that in the nightmare I seemed to be up in the air, flying above the mountains. Even more frightening was what was on the ground. As far as I could see, what looked like a giant map stretched in every direction.

Now I've lived in Tenochtitlan* all my life. There's nothing I don't know about our capital, the greatest city in the Aztec empire, but what I was looking down at in my nightmare was not Tenochtitlan – no way José (where did I hear that?).

* Mexico City

It seemed as if Tenochtitlan had just disappeared. I didn't recognize a thing. If I'd been a god flying to the city I'd have been completely lost.

Our ancestors built Tenochtitlan on an island in the middle of Lake Texcoco. There are causeways built above the water that join the city to the shore of the lake. But the causeways had gone and the lake had vanished. I couldn't believe my eyes.

'Quite a sight, isn't it?' said the nightmare voice again. 'That's the largest city on earth down there. Now put your belt on, please.'

Suddenly there was a tight pull across my tummy. I couldn't move. 'Oh, no,' I thought. 'Someone is really going to cut my heart out with a stone knife this time.'

Then I woke up.

No *pulque* for me today.

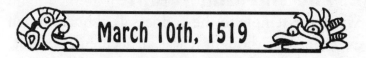

March 10th, 1519

I'm still worried about that nightmare. I've been having the same one on and off since the beginning of the year.

I was tossing and turning on the floor last night thinking about it. Some very strange things have been going on and I'm not the only person in the empire to have noticed.

I have a bad feeling that soon I might need to remember all the things I've been seeing. I'm going to make a list of them here.

1. The Comet

There was that bright star that appeared in the sky. I know it was ten years ago, but I didn't like the look of it then. Nor did our Great Speaker, Montezuma II – Monty for short. When the other soothsayers told him not to worry about that star, or comet, or whatever it was, he had them all killed. I'm glad I kept my mouth shut.

2. The Burning Temple

When the temple to the goddess Toci burnt down, everyone else thought it was an accident, but not our Great Speaker. He saw it as a warning from the gods. He ordered a whole lot more priests and fortune-tellers to be killed and their families sold as slaves.

3. The Day of the Waves

Then there was that terrible day when the lake suddenly turned into massive waves that bashed down houses by the shore. What made it really scary was that the waves rose up without any wind. They just happened. Montezuma didn't like that one little bit. By now he thought the gods really had it in for us all.

4. The Nights of Wailing

After that, things just seemed to get worse, as far as I could see. It's my job to look into the future to find what's going to happen. There were nights when I didn't get a wink of sleep because of the non-stop wailing. You don't have to be a soothsayer to know that wailing is a sure sign of trouble ahead.

5. The Bird with the Mirror

Montezuma got a terrible fright when he was brought that extraordinary bird. It had a mirror in its head – I'll never forget *that* as long as I live. (At this rate I'm going to be very busy trying to live as long as possible. Monty is a bit too keen when it comes to offering other people to the gods as human sacrifices.)

When Monty looked into the mirror in this bird's head he could see stars shining, even though it was daytime. That wasn't all. He also saw lines of men marching to war, but they weren't like men any of us had seen before. They were huge – half men and half deer! It still makes me go cold when I think about it.

By now I'd learnt to keep my lips tightly shut. Thank goodness I'm not a nobleman, otherwise I wouldn't be able to do this because my lips would be plugged with heavy gold jewellery.

'Now look here,' Monty would say. I wish he wouldn't say that because no-one is supposed to look right at him. It's a cut-your-heart-out-up-the-pyramid job for anyone who does. 'Look here,' he'd say. 'What's all this about?'

I mumbled about having to study the stars to be sure, and then something else would happen and he'd forget he'd ever asked me.

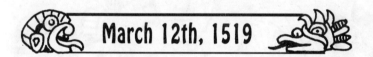

March 11th, 1519

I feel sorry for the peasant who came all the way
to Tenochtitlan, from the coast, to tell Monty
about the peculiar thing he'd seen. This peasant
must have had too much sun or too much *pulque*,
because when he got here he told a crazy story
about watching a huge mountain moving through
the sea. I can understand why Monty had him
locked up. You've got to be careful what you say
round here. You can't have people walking round
the empire talking about floating mountains.

Whatever next?

March 12th, 1519

I wrote too soon. I had another dream last night.
Those floating mountains are real… and they've
brought gods with them!

I dreamt that gods with pale, hairy faces had
landed. Gods with hard metal skins. The wooden-
walled mountains they came in are out on the
water – our canoes look tiny alongside them.

It must be the god Quetzalcoatl. He has
returned, just as the ancient prophecy said he

would. In the olden days, Quetzalcoatl disappeared over the water to the east, promising to come back in the year One Reed. This year is One Reed (that's another thing I know as a soothsayer) and now it looks as if Quetzalcoatl has come back – with a band of servants. Some of the servants are the half-man, half-deer monsters that Monty saw in the bird mirror.

It looks as if all the bad signs meant something. If it is the god Quetzalcoatl, he'll be coming back here to rule his old kingdom. What's Monty going to do about that?

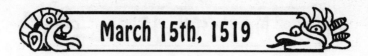

Monty is sending a group of important nobles to meet the pale hairy-faced gods. He's sending me along too. It looks as if I might end up as a sacrifice sooner than I expected.

I've never been down to the sea before. I should be as happy as a lizard on a sunny rock, but I've got serious doubts about this particular trip to the beach. For one thing it's a long hard walk for many days through the mountains before the road drops down to the coast. Then, merchants who've been there tell me, it's very hot and sweaty down by the sea.

On top of that, we'll have to travel through country belonging to people we've conquered. Monty has had lots of wars against them, in fact he seems to fighting *someone* most of the time. Monty makes these conquered people pay tribute to us every year. I don't think we Aztecs are flavour of the month outside the empire.

Or maybe we are. Some people say you can't beat a nice piece of prisoner flesh for a tasty snack. The palm of the hand is supposed to be especially delicious.

March 30th, 1519

Well, we made it to the coast. The merchants were right. It is hot and sweaty. Tenochtitlan is high up on a plateau. Days are hot and dry in the city but the nights can be cold. Down here, by the sea, it seems to be hot all the time. But why am I writing about the weather after what I've seen today?

I must ask Monty to release the peasant who told him about the floating mountains, unless he's already had his heart cut out to keep the gods happy. Those floating mountains he talked about *are* definitely real. I know because I went on one today!

We paddled out in canoes to get to it and down on the water those wooden sides look as high as a temple. Some of the god's servants helped us climb up onto the mountain where there was a flat surface like the top of a pyramid, but made of wood. Up above, the mountain has tall trees with branches sticking out at the side and ropes everywhere. I've never seen so many ropes.

Once we were on the mountain, our nobles straightened their headdresses and went forward to meet the god. The funny thing was that he didn't look that different from us. OK, his face was whiter and he had hair round his chin, and the skin round the top part of his body was hard and gleamed just like metal in the sun.

But he spoke to his servants in the manner we do, though I couldn't understand what he said, of course. He moved like we do, too. I thought a god would fly. This god was a bit of a letdown in some ways.

Monty had sent the god some fabulous presents; baskets filled with precious jewels, gold figures, beautiful capes, headdresses, fans with the best green feathers you can find in the Aztec empire. He even sent a complete Quetzalcoatl outfit so that the pale-faced hairy god could dress up to look the way a god should.

The god's servants didn't exactly call him Quetzalcoatl, though. The name they used sounded like, Corkscrews... Corpsés... Cortés – something like that.

None of us could understand a word he said. But luckily there was a woman who could speak to the god as well as to us. She said the god called her Doña Marina. Although she was an Indian like us, she must have learnt to speak the language of the gods. So she translated what our nobles said to the god, and what the god said to them.

The god seemed to like the gold presents and wanted to know where he could get some more.

Our nobles asked if the god was going to travel to our capital, Tenochtitlan. He said yes, once he had organized his camp here on the coast. I don't think Monty will be too pleased to hear that.

Then our nobles pricked themselves with cactus spines to draw blood, the way we always do to be polite to the gods. But this god didn't like that, especially when he was offered some of the blood in a cup. He started beating the noble who handed it to him with the flat part of the shiny metal stick

hanging from his belt. He got really angry, shouting at us that that we shouldn't touch human blood. But why not?

The next thing we knew, he had us tied up. Then one of the hollow metal tree trunks that shoots fire exploded. I thought a volcano was erupting. The noise was deafening and we all fell down, covered in a cloud of smoke.

The god let us go after that and we paddled off in our canoes as fast as we could. Tomorrow we set off back to Tenochtitlan to tell Monty what's happened. He won't like it. I know he won't.

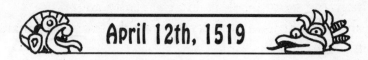

I was right. Monty didn't like it when he heard what had happened to us. I let the others do the talking, just in case he decided to send them up the pyramid to the temple priests, to have their hearts cut out.

Monty called a meeting of the supreme council to decide what to do. I wasn't there, of course.

Only the top people in the empire belong to the supreme council – people like the Woman Snake, the second most important person after Monty. I've often wondered why the Woman Snake is called that, because she isn't a woman at all. The Woman Snake is a man. Do other people feel as muddled, I wonder?

The supreme council decided to be nice to this god, but that he must be stopped from coming to Tenochtitlan.

June 27th, 1519

I had another nightmare last night. I saw the hairy god and his few hundred servants marching through the mountains on the way to Tenochtitlan. I could see their faces clearly, as they passed me. But after the last of them had gone, I knew why I've had a nasty worried feeling for so long. Following them was a massive army of Indians!

They weren't people from Monty's empire. They came from the places that send us tributes every year: all the pretty coloured feathers, the striped blankets, the thousands of balls of tree-

gum, the gold, the silver, the jewellery, the lip plugs and nose plugs made from precious stones, the paper made from tree bark that we use for our books, not to mention the slaves – all the things that make an Aztec's life worth living.

In my nightmare these people had joined up with the hairy god and his servants. They were on their way to fight against us. There were thousands and thousands of them, stretching back down the road as far as I could see.

I wanted to run back to Tenochtitlan to warn Monty. But my legs wouldn't move. Then I felt warm breath on my face. It was terrible! I was staring at the head of a half-man, half-deer monster and it was about to eat me. I could feel its wet tongue on my cheek…

Then I woke up screaming.

It was Feedo, the hairless dog with no bark which I keep in the yard with Gobbl Gobbl, the turkey that gives me eggs. I call all my dogs Feedo. Of course I can't afford to eat dogs as often as Monty does, but they do make a nice treat on a special occasion. I think this one's heading for the cooking pot soon, after the fright he gave me last night.

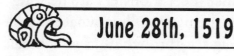

June 28th, 1519

Now I think I'm having a daymare.

Some of Monty's tax collectors have just come back from the coast with a terrible story. They were sent down there to fetch tributes in the usual way. But instead, they were taken prisoner by the people. The hairy god and his servants were in the town and the local people have sided with them against Monty and the rest of us.

My nightmare's coming true after all. The next thing I know they'll be on their way here. Then what shall we do?

August 10th, 1519

They are coming!

They left the coast two days ago, so the runner says. He jogged into the city today carrying the message in the split stick that messengers use. Monty's spies say hundreds of Indians are with the hairy god and his army.

The half-man, half-deer monsters are heading this way. Some of them are pulling what look like tables riding on big see-through discs which roll along the road. The messenger said people had heard the hairy god's servants calling the discs 'wheels'. What on earth can they be?

I've been feeling too depressed to write anything in this diary for ages. News has come in most days from the spies about the hairy god and his army. Whoever is leading them here is taking them a long way round, but it doesn't seem to have put him off, more's the pity.

However, today's news is so bad I must write it down. The hairy god and his small army have fought battles against the great armies of our enemies, the Tlaxcalans, and they have won every one of them! Now the people of Tlaxcala have joined the hairy god and the other Indians to fight against us.

Monty's armies have never won a war against the Tlaxcalans, but the spies say it only took a few of the half-men, half-deer monsters, and the metal tree trunks that shook fire, to scare them away.

The shiny metal sticks they use are powerful weapons too. Our clubs with sharp, jagged chips of stone fitted along the edges don't seem much use against them. The big difference in these battles is that the hairy god and his army *kill* as many of the enemy as they can. Aztecs don't fight battles to do that. The whole point of battles is to capture prisoners, so that the priests can sacrifice them to the gods, to thank the gods for the suffering *they* had when they made the world. The priests get through thousands of sacrifices every year. If we didn't have prisoners to offer, I know who'd soon be climbing up the temple steps to say goodbye to this world. And I want to stay around for a good long time yet.

The only good news is that the Tlaxcalans killed the deer parts of two of the half-men, half-deer monsters. If they can be *killed*, they can't be gods, because the gods cannot die. Maybe there's hope for we Aztecs after all.

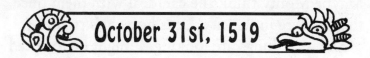

October 31st, 1519

More bad news.

A message has come from Cholula, the holy city about eighty miles away. Hundreds of people have been killed by the hairy god's army and the Indians fighting with them. What makes it even more frightening is that they were killed in the temple of Quetzalcoatl himself. If the hairy god is Quetzalcoatl, what's he doing killing the lords and people of Cholula in his own temple? And if he isn't the god Quetzalcoatl, who is he?

Monty's in a total panic. There's nothing we can do to stop them marching right into Tenochtitlan.

Maybe Monty thinks he can deal with them once they're here in the city. Let's hope he's right.

The way things are looking, I might be tempted to go up the pyramid to offer *myself* to the priests as a sacrifice. Some people do and they get a great send off, with fabulous feasting and parties and all the riches and comfort they want before they go.

That sounds a better way to make my journey to the gods than fighting against the hairy god with his terrible fire-shooting tree trunks and shiny metal fighting sticks.

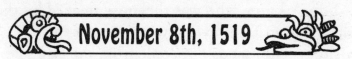

November 8th, 1519

After all the waiting and all the messages from spies along the way, the hairy god, his army and the Indians that have been fighting with them have arrived. They left the coast nearly three months ago. They have fought and beaten our strongest enemies on the way and now they are here, in Tenochtitlan. I think I need several cups of *pulque*.

Monty went out to meet them himself. I had to go along too, though I wasn't thrilled at the idea. I could smell the danger.

I don't know who was the most amazed by the sight that met our eyes – we Aztecs or the visitors. Thousands of people from the capital and the towns around the shores of the lake paddled their canoes beside the straight causeways to stare at them, as the hairy god and his followers marched towards the city. All the Aztecs were terrified by the half-man, half-deer creatures, especially having seen that the hairy god had turned into one. But he suddenly turned into a man again and jumped down onto the ground to stand by the half-deer part, which was as tall as he was.

The visitors seemed pretty surprised by what they saw. Tenochtitlan *is* quite a sight with its tall pyramids and rich palaces. The city looks like a jewel, surrounded by the water of the lake. Then there are the smaller cities and towns all round the shore with their little green fields raised above the water, and people *everywhere*. There are more than 250,000 people living in Tenochtitlan alone.

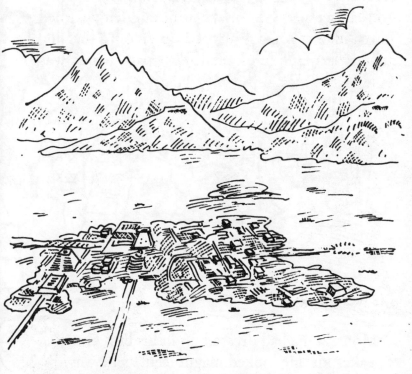

No wonder the hairy god and his followers looked surprised. Oh, yes – we Aztecs are a pretty amazing bunch!

Montezuma had dressed up in his best Great
Speaker kit. He looked magnificent as he was
carried by four Aztec lords, under a covering of
green feathers decorated with gold, silver and
pearls. When he got out of his chair we could see

his sandals with gold soles. But they never
actually touched the ground because servants put
down mats for him to walk on. None of us dared
look at his face, of course, but we all sneaked
glances when he went by.

The hairy god was standing by the half-deer monster when Monty reached him. Marina, the Indian woman I'd met at the coast, translated what they said to each other. It was all very polite. The hairy god put a necklace of coloured beads strung on a golden cord round Monty's neck. I thought we were in for a spot of bother when he went to give Monty a hug. But the Aztec lords stopped him just in time. It does seem an odd way for a god to behave.

Anyhow, Monty welcomed him and invited him to stay in one of the poshest palaces in Tenochtitlan – the one Monty's dad had lived in, no less. It's one of the best palaces in the city, in one of the best areas, right beside the grand square in the centre of the city, close to the great pyramid where the sacrifices take place. It's built of stone and it's two storeys high, unlike my little home that's made of dried mud and has just the one room. I hope our Great Speaker knows what he's doing letting the god and his servants move in here, right in the centre of the city.

To thank Monty, the hairy god's servants exploded two of their metal tree trunks which burst with a great roar, shooting out flame and smoke. Being a soothsayer I guessed that this would happen, but everyone else was terrified. I don't suppose anyone will get a wink of sleep tonight.

November 9th, 1519

After the nightmares and everything else that's happened since the first news arrived about the hairy god, I'd been expecting something bad to happen to me. Now it has – in a big way.

Monty ordered me into his palace late last night and told me that I've got to be the official guide to the hairy god and his army. It's my job, as a soothsayer, to find out what they want to see, then show them.

November 10th, 1519

I knew it! The hairy god wants to know all about our great city and its treasures. It's a good job we've just had a new brochure written by Brainboxl, chief historian to the Great Speaker.

Welcome to...

TENOCHTITLAN

The Heart of the Aztec Empire

Legends tell us that our great capital was founded by the first Aztecs to explore the beautiful Lake of Texcoco. For many generations the Aztecs, the people from Aztlan, had been looking for a new home. They were encouraged by their god Blue Hummingbird (Huitzilopochtli to his local followers) to make their new home where they saw an eagle with a snake in its mouth, sitting on a cactus. One day they came to an island in Lake Texcoco and saw what Blue Hummingbird had foretold.

I hope Marina can translate this into the hairy god's language. I don't think I'm going to be much good at talking to him and I'm scared stiff of what he might do to me if he doesn't like something I tell him, or show him.

Trust Monty to dump this on me.

There was an eagle with a snake in its beak sitting on a cactus. Their search for a new home was over.

Today the island has grown into a great city — but its name reminds us of that historic beginning. Tenochtitlan means 'the place of the fruit of the cactus'.

I don't know where we'd be without Marina. She must be a genius. I expect the hairy god and his friends think so too. If it wasn't for her, they wouldn't have anything to eat or drink. Everyone in the city was too frightened to go near them so no-one took them any food. It was only when Marina persuaded people that the hairy god really wouldn't hurt them, that food started arriving.

No-one knew what they liked eating. So all sorts of delicious things were served and someone had thoughtfully sprinkled fresh blood over the tastiest food, straight from the sacrifice the priests had made up at the pyramid temple.

But they all refused to touch any of the food that had human blood on it.

If Marina hadn't sorted things out, there could have been big trouble. She explained to me that the hairy god has this thing about blood, in fact he's dead against anything to do with cutting out people's hearts. That seems strange after all the Indians that his army has killed fighting their way here. But there you go. He's just one of heaven's great mysteries.

Anyhow, I put two and two together and before you could say Huitzilopochtli, I shot out to a place that serves the best Aztec food I know to get them something else to eat. I've kept the menu in case we have any more trouble in the future.

★ -TEXCOOKO- ★
Take-Away

Our specialities (Everything's cooked to a 'T')

TADPOLES   TOMATOES

TAMALE DUMPLINGS   TURKEY

       TAPIRS

THICK SOUPS   TLAXCALLI TORTILLAS

Other tempting Tenochtitlan treats:

Armadillo - Deer - Duck
Hairless Barkless Dog ('A bite
that's better than its bark')
Fish Frog Lizard Wild rabbit.

ECONOMY DISHES, FOR EVERYDAY EATING
('Its like eating for free')

Beans   Cactus   Sweet potatoes

Chillies   Fish Eggs

Insect larvae   Grubs   Peanuts

Texcooko's
top tipples:
   Pumpkin   Snails

Chocolate made from real cocoa beans
('Only for the seriously rich')
Pulque ('Everyone's favourite')

At least the hairy god and his friends aren't hungry any more, after all the food I took them yesterday.

I'm not sure about the half-deer monsters. They're so big, and so frightening, the way they blow through their noses and stamp about on their four huge feet. I made sure that they got nice juicy bits of dog and turkey and piles and piles of tortillas. But they only sniffed at these. What they really liked were the ordinary raw vegetables.

As for the chocolate drink, they smashed the pottery bowls when they trod on them and then drank the washing water out of the bowl.

I ask you! There's no pleasing some gods.

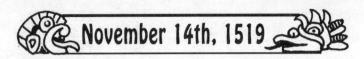

November 14th, 1519

Sightseeing today – another disaster!

Monty told me to put on a good show for the hairy god, so I had a word with the temple priests and they cut out a big, juicy heart from a sacrifice just as we climbed the top steps of the holy pyramid.

I could tell things weren't going too well when the hairy god and his friends started holding their noses as we walked up to the temple platform. You'd think as gods they'd appreciate the smell of old blood that covers the top steps. But you'd

never guess that from
the way they looked.
Anyone would think they
were walking past the barges
where we all do our 'business',
before the 'business' we've done gets taken out to
the fields in the lake to be spread on the crops to
make them grow well.

Normally, when visitors get to the top of the
pyramid (visitors who aren't sent up as sacrifices
that is), they usually marvel at the view. This is
the highest place in Tenochtitlan and from here
you can look right out across the city. The closest
buildings are the royal palaces and the other
temples to the
gods. These stand
round the central
square.

In the sunlight the white walls gleam and shine like silver, in fact some of the hairy god's servants thought they were made of silver. That's all they seem to be interested in – gold and riches.

As you look further away you see the houses where the craftsmen live. Every visitor wants to take home some special Aztec souvenirs. Some of us hope these particular visitors will be heading home very soon.

Beyond the craftsmen's houses you see the thousands of homes belonging to the ordinary people – neat, flat-roofed mud houses just like

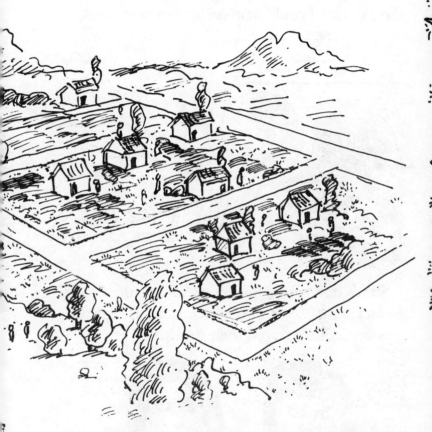

mine, with a little yard outside where people keep their animals and grow vegetables. Then you get to the lake and the four big causeways that run like straight white ribbons across the brown water, joining the city with the shore.

There's also a stone pipe which brings water to Tenochtitlan all the way from the mountains in the distance. I'm glad that was built before my time. Knowing my luck, Monty would have made me a slave so that I could help on the building work.

Slaves don't have houses or land of their own. In fact slaves don't have much at all, except the wooden collars round their necks.

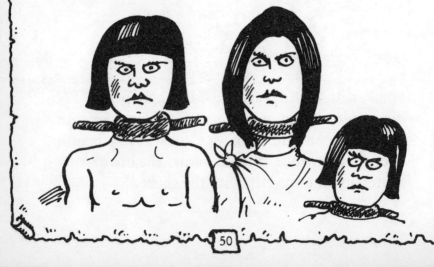

Some slaves are captured in fighting against other cities and a lot of those end up with a one-way walk to the top of the temple pyramid. Other people sell themselves and their families as slaves when they don't have enough to eat in times of famine. Famine can be a big problem when 250,000 people live on an island where everything has to be carried in on porters' backs across the causeways, or paddled in by canoe.

In the distance are the towns and cities around the shore of the lake, and far away, surrounding the whole valley, are the mountains and volcanoes. Tenochtitlan is certainly quite a sight.

But the hairy god and his friends seemed much more interested in the temple where the statues of the gods live, and the place where the priests cut out hearts and burn them as offerings to the gods. The hairy god got very cross at what he saw. Perhaps it was because he couldn't see a statue of himself. He began shouting about some other god called Jesus (I think that was his name) and his mother (was her name Mary?).

Our priests told him that he must be getting muddled, because there are no gods round here with names like that.

Then the hairy god made them angry by saying that this Jesus god was also the son of god and that he and his Dad were the only real gods. He even went as far as saying that they should have their own special place of worship in the temple on the pyramid. He wants to put a cross made of wood there. Really! What sort of a god does he think he is? It wouldn't surprise me if the hairy god doesn't turn out to be some sort ordinary person called Senõr Courtyard... Courtship..., Cortés... or whatever his servants call him. He's Senõr Caught-out if you want my opinion.

November 20th, 1519

I think Monty's starting to have his own doubts about Caught-out.

Yesterday the hairy god took him prisoner! He took Montezuma II, the Great Speaker, prisoner right here in his own capital.

Monty is telling everyone that he's chosen to stay in the hairy god's palace. But I know the truth. Caught-out may be letting Monty have his servants, and hundreds of nice things to eat every day, just as he does in his own palace. But Monty can't leave, even if he wants to. Caught-out has made him his prisoner and I think I'm the only person in Tenochtitlan to realize this.

I was really worried there might be big trouble today. This is the time of year when our brave warriors hold major celebrations at the great pyramid in honour of the god Huitzilopochtli and his victory over Coyolxauhqui. These celebrations always need masses of sacrifices and I thought that Caught-out might cause trouble when he saw what was going on.

Today I noticed that many of the warriors had changed their hairstyles since the last celebrations. Some of the young ones have cut the long lock of hair they have to wear until they capture their first prisoner; so they've made a good start. Others are now wearing their hair tied up which shows that they've captured at least three prisoners.

The good thing about being a successful warrior is that you can be rewarded with expensive gifts, and if you're really brave and capture lots of prisoners Monty and the other nobles might make you a higher ranking person. That can't be bad, can it?

I've always been useless at fighting. 'Dream, dream, dream. Is that all you ever do?' my dad used to complain. He was right, of course. That's why I'm a soothsayer. But at least I know a bit about the army and fighting because I have to look into the future to decide when it's a good time to fight a war.

The warriors who always impress me are the jaguar knights. They dress in jaguar skins, with helmets like jaguar heads, and they go into battle at night. This takes courage, because most Aztecs are scared stiff of going out after dark when spirits are on the prowl. The eagle knights are also top warriors – they go into battle at dawn. They are dressed like eagles and they'd certainly put the fear of death into me if I was fighting against them.

When they're still boys, warriors in the Aztec army start learning to use a long wooden club fitted with sharp chips of obsidian* rock. These can hack through really tough material so lots of our warriors wear padded cotton armour, soaked in salt water to make it stiff. (I notice that some of Caught-out's servants have started wearing it too, instead of the shiny metal skins they had when they arrived.) The only problem with the obsidian chips is that they snap off and break too easily. I don't think Caught-out's bright metal fighting sticks can be damaged in that way.

All our other weapons were on display during the celebrations: bows and flint-tipped arrows; spears which our warriors use with throwing sticks that send them flying a very long way; slings that hurl stones even further; and hundreds of beautiful shields decorated with lovely feather shapes and pictures.

This celebration with thousands of armed warriors is always a great sight. Maybe that's why Caught-out didn't try to start any trouble.

*volcanic

Monty's still convinced that Caught-out is a god, despite what's happened. At least he doesn't agree with Caught-out about the Jesus god he keeps talking about. Monty says he doesn't mind staying with Caught-out if it makes him happy, and to keep him happy we all went to the match today.

I don't know what sort of games Caught-out plays, but he obviously hasn't seen a game of *tlachtli** before. He kept going on about a game he knows in which players kick the ball with their feet. This doesn't sound very interesting to me. I suppose you can't expect much from a game with a boring name like 'football'.

Today's game was between the league champions, the Temple Tigers, and the Cactus Eagles. A big crowd turned out to support both sides and I was glad that Monty had given us the best place to watch the game, otherwise we wouldn't have been able to see much. We were on raised steps overlooking the middle of the ball-court. On each side of the playing area there are high stone walls and halfway along each wall (right in front of us) there is a stone ring set high in the wall about twice the height of a man from

*Aztec ball game

the ground. The walls are about ten man-paces apart and from one end to the other the playing area is about sixty man-paces long. So the players have to be very fit to keep going.

Tlachtli is a real test of skill. The players can only hit the ball with their elbows, hips, bottoms and knees. I've had a go at doing this and it isn't easy. It's also very painful. I had some huge bruises afterwards and some players get badly injured (even killed). Sometimes the losers are sacrificed, that's why everyone tries really hard to win.

The winners can get great prizes: coloured feathers and other expensive things. They can even be given the clothes worn by the spectators! I'm glad that didn't happen after the game we watched – I didn't fancy walking back to the palace naked!

January 3rd, 1520

Caught-out has been showing a lot of interest in our merchants lately. Aztec merchants are a funny lot. They have their own gods, their own laws and their own customs. They never wear expensive clothes and most of them are very secretive about what they trade and bring back here. No-one knows how rich they really are. My dreams tell me that they are very rich and very powerful. That's why the nobles don't like them. They're frightened the merchants are actually richer and more powerful than they are.

Merchants are about the only people, except for tax collectors and warriors, who are allowed to travel away from Tenochtitlan. So merchants are very useful spies for Monty because they see what's going on in all the places where they go to trade. As well as bringing wonderful things back from all parts of the country, they bring back lots of valuable information which Monty, the Woman Snake and the rest of the supreme council use to plan the next war. Monty is at war so often he needs new information all the time.

This is the month when the merchant traders have their big religious festival but I don't think Caught-out is particularly interested in that.

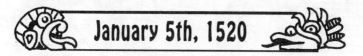 **January 5th, 1520**

Caught-out seems extremely keen for me to take him to the market today. I wonder if he wants to find something out from the merchants too?

We have markets every few days in Tenochtitlan and thousands of people come to them. Caught-out kept asking me for something he called 'money'. I didn't know what he meant. Then Marina explained. Apparently Caught-out and his servants use this money stuff to get things they want at markets. Marina says it looks like small discs of gold and silver. It seems a funny way of doing business.

Why don't they barter and swap things like we do? If someone wants a canoe, they give the person with the canoe a few blankets and the canoe becomes theirs. Other people swap expensive things like feathers for other expensive things like precious stones, or gold and silver, or slaves.

Who needs this money
stuff? It sounds awfully
complicated to me. If there's a
bit of a difference between the
things that have been swapped,
people make up the difference with
cocoa beans, or some gold dust kept in the hollow
quill of a goose feather. The system has worked
perfectly well here for as long as anyone can
remember. Trust a stranger to want to change it.

When we arrived at the market, Marina
whispered to me that Caught-out and his servants
had never seen a market this size. There are
usually 20,000 people here, so I suppose we have
got used to it, but the strangers said it was the
biggest market they had ever been to.

You can get everything you want here from
fruit and vegetables to the sharpest stone knives
and the biggest selection of coloured feathers in
the world.

Caught-out is very crafty, if you ask me. He
wanted to know which merchant had most
recently come back from the coast, so that he
could find out what was happening in the country
he'd come through on his way here.

It turned out that Stinkingrichl arrived last night
from a long journey in that area, so Caught-out
took Marina and spent a long time talking to him.

I didn't see him showing much interest in what Stinkingrichl had brought back, until he showed Caught-out pearls and gold. Then old 'hairy-chop's' eyes really lit up. I wonder what he gave Stinkingrichl for those treasures?

Caught-out looked very pleased with himself when he left Stinkingrichl. I hung around a nearby stall trying to hear what they were talking about. I got so tired waiting I sat down, and jumped right up again with a terrible jabbing pain in my backside. I should have known better, it was a maguey cactus stall and I'd just sat on a stack of prickly cactus leaves!

The stall keeper wanted me to give him something for them, because he said no-one would want them after I'd sat on them. I told him I'd think about it and he gave me this bit of tree bark paper about his stall as a reminder.

Montezuma
CACTUS

By Royal Appointment to our Great Speaker Montezuma II

Suppliers of all sorts of things made from Maguey cactus

(including more pulque than anyone, except old people, should ever drink)

Among our leading brands, why not try:

Cactus leaf fuel for home heating and cooking

Cactus leaf thatching for the roof over your head

Cactus leaf mats to decorate your homes

Cactus leaf baskets, so useful around the house and the market

Cactus leaf cloth for the clothes you wear (spun from the finest maguey cactus fibres, but only suitable for the common people and slaves)

Cactus spines for sewing, stitching, drawing blood and punishing the kids

Delicious maguey cactus pulque to make every day a right royal day for the elderly and carefree.

Now that we're in the last month of the year, Caught-out has noticed that grown-ups are going round pulling children by the neck. I could see him starting to get worked up about this, so I moved in quickly before he began making a fuss and told him that this is the month which celebrates growth. All the grown-ups are doing is helping the children grow. It's as simple as that.

Caught-out didn't look convinced, so Marina suggested that we paid a visit to a couple of schools, so that he could see how well Aztec children are educated and taught to behave. Caught-out liked the sound of that and today we started at my local *telpochalli**.

I don't have any kids of my own, because soothsayers and priests aren't allowed to get married but I teach fortune-telling in this particular *telpochalli*, which is organized by the *calpulli*.**

*neighbourhood boys' school
** neighbourhood clan

From the age of eight the boys start learning
how to fight like warriors. They also have lessons
in useful subjects like farming, fishing, pottery,
building, carpentry, making canoes – the sorts of
things they'll need to know about when they
become grown-up, although they all know what
work they will be doing when they become men,
because most ordinary Aztec men always do the
same jobs as their fathers.

Unfortunately, while we were at the school, it was punishment time. Two of the boys had been fighting in class, so one of them was held by a teacher over a fire of burning chillies that made him cough and his eyes water, while the other one had cactus spines stuck into him to teach him a lesson.

I thought Caught-out might get the wrong
idea about what was going on, but he seemed
to understand the need to be strict with children;
he even asked if he could have a go at sticking in
some of the spines.

Caught-out didn't seem very interested in girls'
education. Maybe it isn't very important where he
comes from. Marina told him that, as they grow up,

girls learn all the things they need to know to run
a home and look after a family: collecting fuel,
cooking, cleaning, weaving, making clothes,
looking after children – things that are much more
important than fighting, according to Marina.

After lunch we went across town to visit the
oldest and most famous school in Tenochtitlan
which is only for the sons of upper-class families,
like myself!

Boys go to this *calmecac** when they are eight years old to be taught how to become future leaders. They sleep on hard floors and the food isn't up to much; sometimes they have nothing to eat for a couple of days to toughen them up. The teachers stick cactus thorns into them so that they get used to pain. They will need to be able to draw their own blood so that they can please the gods. It's nice to see the old traditions still going strong.

*school for male children of noblemen

For lessons the boys are taught the history of
the Aztecs; reading, writing and astronomy (my
best subject at school). They are also taught about
law and government for the time when they
become leaders themselves. There are lessons in
fighting and warfare too. Those were my worst
subjects, but I knew that I wouldn't be a warrior.

I went to the lessons for boys who were going to be priests, where we were taught why we need to make sacrifices to thank the gods for all they have done for us. But I wasn't much good at sacrificing the small animals we practised on. I failed my practical sacrifice exams so I became a soothsayer because I *was* brilliant at dreaming!

$\frac{10}{10}$ for Dreaming

In one of the classes we visited, the boys were having a writing lesson. I was very pleased to see that the boys still learn to write in the good old Aztec way, with pictures to show the words they are using. This sort of writing is bright and colourful, just as writing should be. It makes history and poetry fun to read and it's helped generations of people like us record everything we've ever needed to know.

Tenochtitlan

tree

stone

Montezuma

Caught-out didn't show much interest in the picture writing lesson. I've seen the way he writes, it looks like tangled cactus thread – all joined up squiggles and circles. I don't think he's a great scholar really. But he *was* interested in the holes the boys had in their lower lips, noses and ear lobes. He knew they had been made to prepare the boys for wearing expensive gold plugs. He kept asking me if I knew who the boys' fathers were, and where they lived. It doesn't take many guesses to understand the reason. Sometimes I think the only reason he came to Tenochtitlan was to find gold.

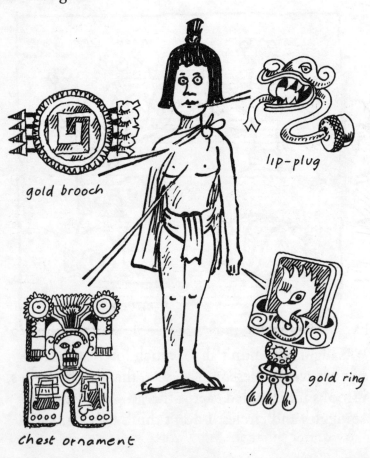

gold brooch

lip-plug

chest ornament

gold ring

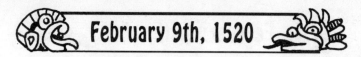

February 9th, 1520

Useless Day number one

The five days at the end of each year are terribly unlucky. No-one does any business. The temples shut down and people fast and lay off the *pulque*.

Everywhere goes quiet and people stay at home to avoid bad luck.

Boring, boring, boring – though at least it has stopped Caught-out prying into things that don't concern him.

I wonder what the New Year will bring?

February 14th, 1520

New Year's Day at last! The year Two Flint has arrived! I thought the five Useless Days would never end. But now life can begin again and we can all look forward to the eighteen months in the farmer's calendar.

To celebrate, Monty took Caught-out and the rest of his hangers-on to watch the flying display. Needless to say Caught-out didn't know the first thing about this and insisted on calling it *volador*; apparently that means 'flyer' in his language. My recurring nightmare is always about flying, so I don't fancy it myself.

'What the heck – hit the deck', people were chanting as the four flying men, dressed as birds and attached to ropes, climbed a tall pole. A fifth man holding a drum was sitting up on the top of the pole. When the others reached him, he started beating the drum as fast as he could. You could feel the excitement growing in the crowd watching on the ground. Then the four birdmen jumped out from the top of the pole and began to swing round it as their ropes unwound.

Caught-out looked totally baffled by what was happening, so we had to explain that each of the men tries to 'fly' round the pole thirteen times before he reached the ground. If Caught-out was

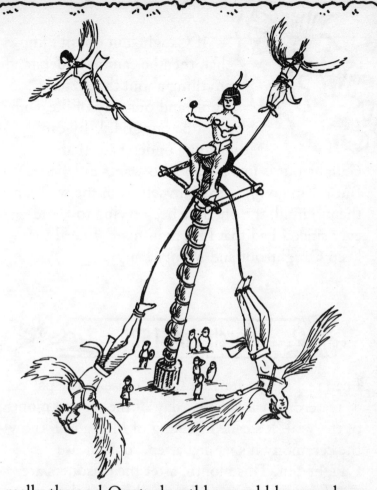

really the god Quetzalcoatl he would know why this was important. Four multiplied by thirteen makes fifty-two, and fifty-two is a magic number to us. Once every fifty-two years the two Aztec calendars – the farmers' calendar and the holy calendar – finish on almost the same day. That's when the world could end and evil spirits could take over from us.

If Caught-out doesn't know that, then he cannot understand anything about the Aztec people and our way of life, so he cannot be our god. Why can't Montezuma understand that Caught-out is just a man who wants our riches? But if I'm going to save myself from the walk up the pyramid, the one I've been trying to avoid ever since I had that first nightmare, I need to keep Caught-out and Monty happy.

March 7th, 1520

I can feel things starting to get tense in the palace.
Yesterday was the first day of the second month of the year. It's called Flaying of Men and I know the ceremony it's named after won't please Caught-out. This month, after the prisoners are sacrificed, the priests take the skins off their bodies and go round wearing them for twenty days. I can just imagine what Caught-out would think of that.

In order to distract him from what the priests
are dressing themselves in, I suggested he might
like to add a few things to his own spring
wardrobe from my new picture catalogue.

First he looked at the clothes for ordinary
people, made from the rough
cloth of cactus fibres: simple
loin-cloths for men, wound
round their middles and
between their legs, and tied
in place with a big knot or
bow.

Caught-out kept muttering about things he called 'buckles' and 'buttons', but I hadn't a clue what he was on about. Aztec clothes have plenty of their own decorations; they don't need any foreign ones. Besides, ordinary people aren't allowed to wear decorations or fancy clothes. The law on this is very strict. Any ordinary person found wearing something like cotton, for example, is sentenced to death.

Ordinary men can't wear nice long flowing cloaks that hang down covering their legs, either. The only exception to this is if a man has legs that have been badly scarred in battle. If that's the case the law lets him wear a long cloak to hide his old wounds. Otherwise if you wear a long cloak when you shouldn't, it's curtains.

The clothes for ordinary women looked pretty much like those I've known women wear all my life. There's the usual long skirt tied at the waist, over which they wear a baggy tunic. Both of these garments are made from cactus-fibre cloth, of course!

Caught-out began to take a serious interest when he got to the pages of clothes for upper-class people, in lovely soft, smooth materials like cotton, which only the very rich could afford. I always think they must make much more comfortable loin-cloths than the ones made from rough cactus fibres.

There were cloaks of dyed cotton decorated with gorgeous brightly coloured feathers, precious stones and gold thread. For cold weather there were warm, cosy cloaks lined with rabbit fur. For hot weather there were brightly coloured sunshades with more gold and feather decorations.

Clothes *NEW*

fur lined

cloak → *NEW*

headdress

loin-cloth →

BIG

check your size

There were pages and pages of displays of jewellery with necklaces, plugs and rings that could be stuck into noses, lips, ears or worn round necks and fingers. No wonder you can tell at a glance which people in Tenochtitlan are rich and powerful.

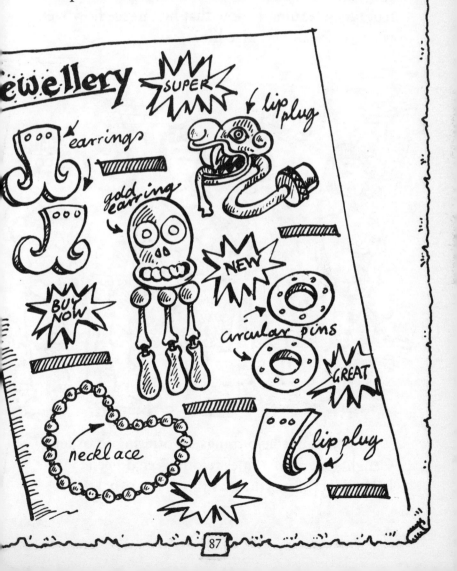

ewellery

SUPER

lip plug

earrings

gold earring

NEW

BUY NOW

circular pins

GREAT

necklace

lip plug

For footwear, only upper-class people can wear sandals. Everyone else goes round with bare feet. You can't run a city or an empire without being able to tell who's an ordinary person and who's a nobleman. Perhaps that's why Caught-out is here. Maybe he thinks he can take over our empire from Montezuma II now that he can see how well we Aztecs can organize life?

Monty didn't help things by offering to order Caught-out all the finest clothes we'd been looking at. Monty knows this is the usual Aztec way of showing off his power and wealth, but I wouldn't mind betting that Caught-out sees it the other way round. I'm sure he believes Monty is being generous because he thinks Caught-out is the powerful and important one.

No good will come of it – that's what gives me sleepless nights.

April 3rd, 1520

The third month of the year is the time for the ceremonial planting of crops. It gave me a good opportunity to get Caught-out away from the city for a while. He's been here five months now; Monty has been his prisoner for most of that time and the people are starting to get rebellious. Trouble is brewing in Tenochtitlan and I thought a visit to the fields might be a good idea.

The first thing Caught-out wanted to know was who owned the land we were visiting. I told him that the only people who actually *owned* their land were nobles who were given captured land by Monty, or whoever else was Great Speaker. These noble land-owners have slaves who do all the work for them. The rest of the land belongs to the clans and people 'borrow' it from them to grow crops and rear animals.

What Caught-out doesn't seem to understand is that land is very precious. When our ancestors settled at Tenochtitlan, the island was almost all rock. It was very difficult to grow any food. All the fields we have now, around the city, around the shores of the lake and on the hillsides are man-made. Generation after generation of farmers have dug the fields and made them fertile, using the same wooden digging sticks and hoes that farmers have been using for a thousand years or more. Who says we can't learn from history?

The laws about farming are very strict. They have to be, to make sure that the right crops are grown at the right time. Anyone who plants seeds before the government tells them to plant is punished.

The fields we went to look at had been created in the lake. The lake isn't very deep, so it was possible to build up land to make fields where there was once only fish, frogs and water plants.

Caught-out didn't understand this, so we paddled our canoes to a place where a new *chinampa** was being made. He saw a rectangular shape, surrounded by a line of poles driven into the bed of the lake. A fence of woven branches had been fitted between the poles. Once these barriers were in place, the workers filled the space inside with mud scooped from the bottom of the lake. This was mixed with rotting plants and dead twigs so it builds up a thick layer of very fertile soil which rises above the level of the water until a new *chinampa* is created. Trees planted round the edge provide strength to the woven-branch walls and help to hold the field together.

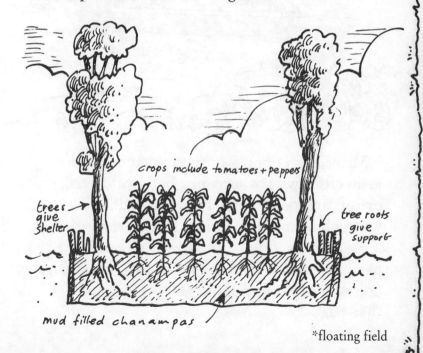

crops include tomatoes + peppers

trees give shelter

tree roots give support

mud filled chanampas

*floating field

For once Caught-out seemed impressed when he looked into the distance at the hundreds of fields that had been made in this way. The narrow canals between them, which the farmers use to move from field to field by canoe, fascinated him too.

Maize, sweet potatoes and tomatoes are the main crops we saw growing, but sunflowers, carrots and peppers are grown as well.

Caught-out was surprised that there weren't more animals. I don't know why – there were plenty of turkeys and dogs. But he made strange noises which sounded like 'Moo-moo' and 'Baa-baa'.

One thing he *did* recognize were the canoes filled with 'business' that had been loaded from the barges floating beside the city. The farmers fetch piles of 'business' each week and paddle it back to their fields to spread it on the soil to make the crops grow. If they didn't do this the soil would soon get tired and the crops wouldn't be able to feed all the people. The crops gives us food. Our food makes the 'business'. The 'business' feeds the soil. And the soil feeds the crops. It's all very well arranged.

Caught-out didn't seem very keen on eating his vegetables at supper last night. I can't think why after a nice day out in the fresh air. He seems to be more grumpy and suspicious than ever.

 May 4th, 1520

The feeling in the city has got much worse in the last month. Caught-out and his army have been here *six* months and the people are getting fed up with them.

Now my dreams tell me that another army of strangers in floating mountains has arrived at the coast. Perhaps they have come to punish Caught-out.

It looks as if the hairy god, whoever he is, may be taken away after all. Brilliant!

 May 5th, 1520

Wrong!

Today Caught-out marched away from the city with eighty of his own warriors and several hundred Indians. He's going down to the coast to fight the new strangers who have just arrived.

I really think the end is in sight for Caught-out. Monty's spies say there are hundreds of warriors in the new army that's just landed. I don't see how he can win against all of them. Monty can't believe his luck. He's like a new man. Caught-out wanted to take Monty with him, but our Great Speaker refused. So Caught-out has left some of his warriors in Tenochtitlan to guard Monty until he gets back – or so he says.

May 17th, 1520

Horror!

This is the feast of Toxcatl, one of the most important Aztec feasts in the whole year. So, what did Caught-out's warriors, who were left here, do? They only attacked and killed hundreds of our nobles and priests while they were celebrating in the Great Temple, here in Tenochtitlan!

There are rumours that some of other Indians from Tlaxcala may have put them up to it by saying that the people in the city were about to attack them. Well, the people of Tenochtitlan are certainly armed and ready to attack them now.

Caught-out's men are surrounded in their palace, with Monty. I had popped out for a quick cup of *pulque*, but I couldn't get back because the streets were filled with fighting warriors. No-one will take them any food now. They'll be starving soon. Serves them right, I say.

The only one I feel sorry for is Monty. He tried to speak to the people from the roof of the palace. He tried to make them understand why he had moved in with Caught-out, but they laughed at him and called him all sorts of horrid names.

No-one would have dared to do that this time last year but things have changed so much since Caught-out landed, I don't think our lives will ever be the same.

I watched Monty from a safe distance. He couldn't believe that his own subjects were turning against him. If it is the end for Caught-out, it could be the end for Montezuma II, our Great Speaker, as well.

How wrong can I be? Call myself a soothsayer?!
Who should come back into the city yesterday
morning as a half-man, half-deer monster, but
Caught-out. Worse still, he's brought even more
warriors with him!

At first I thought he must have used some
strange magic to turn the few warriors he took
with him into this much bigger army. However, it
seems he captured hundreds of the warriors he'd

gone to fight and then asked them to fight for him. Now his army is bigger than when he arrived seven months ago.

Mind you, the city was different for this arrival. All the people stayed indoors. The streets were empty and there was an eerie quiet everywhere.

The warriors who killed all the people in the Great Temple look half starved. They have had almost nothing to eat since the massacre and they had to dig a well to get water. They were pleased to see Caught-out and his army, but no-one else was.

The people of the city have surrounded the palace once again and now Caught-out and all his warriors are trapped inside. They'll really be for it now. What a sacrifice they will make!

Poor old Monty, bad luck seems to stick to him like gum from the rubber tree.

Today there was more heavy fighting round the palace and Caught-out told Monty to go up on the roof to talk to the people and stop them attacking him and his warriors.

Monty wasn't too keen on the idea after the last time he'd tried it. But he went up as he was told. As soon as he appeared the people began yelling at him. He tried to make himself heard above the noise. Then they started throwing stones at him.

He made an easy target and almost immediately he was hit on the head and knocked over.

Caught-out told his medicine man to look after Monty, but things don't look too good. I forsee that our Great Speaker will be saying hello to the gods before me.

I was right. Montezuma II, the Great Speaker, went to join the gods today. He didn't seem to want to recover from the wound to his head. I've got so used to him being around. I don't think a day has gone by when I haven't worried that he might send me up the pyramid to pay a final visit to the gods and now he's gone himself. What will happen to us all now?

Caught-out says he is really sorry, but I wonder if he is. If it hadn't been for him, none of this would have happened.

Monty's body has been taken from the palace to the ceremonial funeral place where all the Great Speakers go. Caught-out wants the people to obey *him* now. Fat chance of that, from what I've seen around the city. There has been hand-to-hand fighting in the streets and several of Caught-out's warriors have been killed, though nothing like as many of our own warriors.

There was a terrible bloody battle at the temple of Yopico, next to the palace where Caught-out has been living. Statues of the gods were destroyed and lots of priests were thrown from the temple at the top. There's no turning back

now. Caught-out's days are numbered. No-one in the city thinks he's a god any more. Maybe something good will come out of all this mess and muddle after all.

July 1st, 1520

They've gone! They've disappeared! Caught-out and most of his warriors turned tail in the night and ran away. I didn't see anything like this happening – not in my wildest dreams.

We didn't let them get away without a real fight. The sneaky pale-skinned rats tried to slip out of the city in the middle of the night. They tied soft material round the big, hard feet of the half-deer monsters so that they wouldn't make a noise on the ground as they escaped. Some of them carried wooden ladders made from roof timbers in the palace. They used them like bridges, to reach across the gaps in the causeway, because we clever Aztecs had taken down the proper bridges to prevent them getting away.

Caught-out must have thought he was terribly clever, escaping in the dark. He knows that only the jaguar warriors and priests go outside at night because of the spirits. However, someone else was out in the city at midnight, a woman fetching water from the lake. She saw them trying to get across their wooden bridge at the first gap in the causeway, just outside the city, and she raised the alarm.

A priest on one of the temple pyramids heard her and started beating a war drum. Soon thousands of our warriors were tumbling out of their houses and into canoes to attack Caught-out and his warriors from both sides of the causeway as they tried to escape.

Who says Aztec warriors can't fight in the dark? Our warriors were magnificent, even though they were fighting in the darkness and shooting arrows from canoes. Caught-out couldn't use his exploding, fire-shooting tree trunks. The half-deer monsters were shrieking with fright. And so many of his warriors fell into the water as they tried crossing from one side of a causeway gap to the other that their bodies filled the gap like a farmer filling his *chinampa* with mud from the bottom of the lake. The last of them were even able to walk over the piled-up bodies of other warriors as they crossed the gap!

More of them would have got away if they hadn't been so greedy. At least it proved one thing – they *are* just interested in gold, jewels and riches. Some of them had so much heavy gold hidden inside their clothes that when they fell in the water they sank straight under the surface and drowned. This morning our warriors found the causeway littered all the way from the city to the shore with treasure Caught-out's army had stolen from the palaces and temples in Tenochtitlan.

I always said we Aztecs would show them a thing or two. And now we have! Goodbye nightmares! Goodbye Caught-out and your warriors! What idiots we were thinking you were a god! Go back to where you came from! That's the last we've seen of you! Goodbye and good riddance!

THE END OF THE AZTECS

Unfortunately Guessalotl's power to see into the future must have failed him at this point. His diary ends here and history loses touch with this remarkable Aztec historian. However, the story of Cortés and the Aztec empire has a twist in the tail.

The Spanish had brought with them the deadly disease called smallpox. The Indians had no resistance to this and thousands died of smallpox after Cortés and his followers had been driven out of the city.

At the end of 1520 Cortés returned to the shores of Lake Texcoco with an even larger army. He was again supported by the Aztec's old enemies, the people of Tlaxcala, and 100,000 Indians were now on his side. Cortés also had 10,000 porters who carried supplies and thirteen small ships that he planned to use to capture Tenochtitlan.

In May 1521 Cortés began his attack on the Aztec capital, approaching the city along the causeways and by water from all sides. Bloody fighting raged for sixty days and nights before Cortés broke into the city.

The Aztec defenders were weak from hunger and disease but they fought fiercely to defend the city street by street as it was gradually destroyed around them. In the end the Spanish invaders and their Indian allies were too strong for them. On 13 August 1520, Cuauhtémoc, the last Great Speaker of the Aztec empire, and nephew of Montezuma II, was taken prisoner. His capture marked the end of Aztec rule. The empire now had new masters and for the next 300 years it formed part of the Spanish empire, until 1821 when it became independent once again, as the country we know today as Mexico.

PUBLISHER'S ADDENDUM

Even though many of the events described in this so-called diary are recorded by reliable historians, a more recent and, we have to say, more thorough study of the book Mr Dickinson found in the market in Spain now makes us believe that it is nothing more than a hoax.

There is no doubt that Montezuma II was the Great Speaker of the Aztecs in the early sixteenth century. Hernán Cortés certainly led the Spanish forces that conquered the Aztec empire. The Indian woman referred to as Doña Marina was genuine and did act as an interpreter for Cortés.

However, it seems very unlikely that Montezuma had a soothsayer with a name like Guessalotl, or that there was a chief historian called Brainboxl and a merchant in Tenochtitlan called Stinkingrichl. We also have serious doubts about the two so-called experts on American history before the arrival of the Spanish. No trace has been found of either Dr Shady Practice or Professor Pulltheotherone.

It is our belief that this hoax has been cooked up to rob an innocent tourist. We only hope he did not pay too much for the 'diary', or for the 'translation' of what now appears to be a picture book for very young children.

It appears that Montezuma may have got his revenge after all.

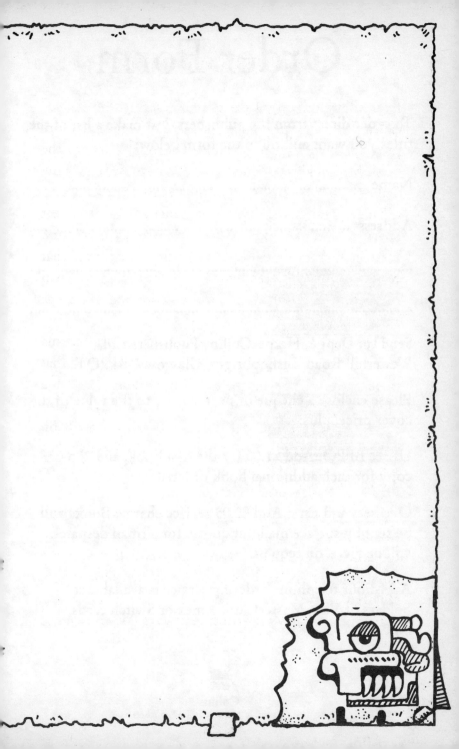

Order Form

To order direct from the publishers, just make a list of the titles you want and fill in the form below:

Name ....

Address ....

....

....

Send to: Dept 6, HarperCollins Publishers Ltd, Westerhill Road, Bishopbriggs, Glasgow G64 2QT.

Please enclose a cheque or postal order to the value of the cover price, plus:

UK & BFPO: Add £1.00 for the first book, and 25p per copy for each additional book ordered.

Overseas and Eire: Add £2.95 service charge. Books will be sent by surface mail but quotes for airmail despatch will be given on request.

A 24-hour telephone ordering service is available to holders of Visa, MasterCard, Amex or Switch cards on 0141- 772 2281.

Collins
An *Imprint* of HarperCollins*Publishers*